This book belongs to

....

For Jane Cameron and everyone at the Acorn and NHP
- thanks for all the years of wonderful No-Snow Days
— R. CURTIS

For Ganfer
— R. COBB

PUFFIN BOOKS

UK | USA | Canada | Ireland | Australia | India | New Zealand | South Africa
Puffin Books is part of the Penguin Random House group of companies whose addresses
can be found at global.penguinrandomhouse.com.

www.penguin.co.uk   www.puffin.co.uk   www.ladybird.co.uk

 Penguin
Random House
UK

First published 2014
This edition published 2020
001

Text copyright © Richard Curtis, 2014
Illustrations copyright © Rebecca Cobb, 2014

The moral right of the author and illustrator has been asserted

A CIP catalogue record for this book is available from the British Library
Printed and bound in China

ISBN: 978–0–241–49245–1

All correspondence to:
Puffin Books, Penguin Random House Children's
One Embassy Gardens, 8 Viaduct Gardens, London SW11 7BW

Snow Day

Written by

Richard Curtis

Illustrated by

Rebecca Cobb

PUFFIN

The date was December the 4th. And no one knew what was about to go down. It was an *ordinary* Wednesday – and the next day was going to be an *ordinary* Thursday.

And all over London Town, children did their homework and went to bed, ready for another long day of school tomorrow.

And then something *miraculous* happened.

During the night, it snowed.
And snowed.
And snowed.

And then it snowed some more.

And in the morning *everything* was white and *everything* was changed.
As the sun rose, every single phone **buzzed** and every single
email **pinged** with the news that there was

NO school today.

Because no one could get into school – not pupils, not teachers,
not gym teachers, not *even* head teachers. **No one**.

Within minutes, the day already had its very special name . . .

It was

Snow Day.

For everyone.

Well, ALMOST everyone – because, at 8.30,
one little boy turned up for school.

His name was **Danny**.

And he was greeted by *one* teacher.

His name was **Mr Trapper**.

And they knew pretty quickly that something
was wrong – because they were *totally* alone.

But there was nothing they could do. Mr Trapper had to stay in the school because there was a pupil there. And Danny had to stay, because his mum and dad were abroad – *as usual* – and his aunt who was taking care of him had left the house at the same time as him, and he had no way of contacting her.

So, Danny and Mr Trapper went inside to begin their day, which was a **pretty bad** situation for the two of them.

Because Danny and Mr Trapper were . . .

ENEMIES.

Mr Trapper was the **strictest** teacher in the school.
And Danny was the **WORST** student in the country.
Well, maybe not the *actual* worst.
But very near the bottom of the bottom of the list.

So the last person Danny wanted to see was Mr Trapper.
And the last person Mr Trapper wanted to see
was that nuisance Danny Higgins.

But they were **stuck** with each other.

For the first lesson, they did **HISTORY**,
during which Danny, as usual, found
it hard to concentrate.

Then came **ENGLISH**, during
which Danny, as usual, found
it hard to *stay awake*.

Then **SCIENCE**, during which
Danny found it impossible
not to fall over.
As always.

Then it was break.

Mr Trapper went outside to smoke his pipe. And Danny went outside to do what every other boy in the country was doing – making enormous snowballs. And then putting them on top of each other, to make a snowman.

But, like lots of boys, he found it wasn't quite as easy as he thought it would be. But then, after the snowman's head had fallen off for the third time, something rather *unexpected* happened.

Mr Trapper **spoke** to him.

"You're doing it wrong," said Mr Trapper.

"I beg your pardon, sir," said Danny, very shocked because it was the first time Mr Trapper had ever said anything to him that wasn't "**Shut Up, Higgins**".

"You've got to slice a bit off the top of the bottom one.
To make the top one stay. Here, have a look."
And Mr Trapper showed him how it was done.
And it *worked*.

Then Mr Trapper did a snowman of his own.
Rather a **good** one.

And then they did a **really massive** one.
Together.

And after that they made
a whole army of snowmen.

Then it was time for **DOUBLE GEOGRAPHY**.
But they built a medieval fort instead.

After which it was lunchtime and they found some sweets
in a craft project in Form 1b. And ate them **ALL**.

Then it was **GAMES** time – and they went
skating, with the help of *Roald Dahl*,
Jane Austen and *Charles Dickens*.

And skied down from the roof,
on Mrs Chattington's *incredibly* useful
one metre rulers.

And then topped it all off with th

...ost *almighty* **snowball fight** of all time.

Then it was the last two lessons.
In MATHS they designed a
very BIG igloo.

In FRENCH, they built it.

And even though the design wasn't perfect – and even though they hardly said a word – they were both

very
happy
indeed.

You see, they both knew a lot about loneliness.

Danny's dad was a really *busy* man – and hardly ever
played with him or asked him any questions at all.

Mr Trapper's dad had been *exactly* the same,
and Mr Trapper never had any kids of his own.

So when the end of the day came and they set off home,
they both knew it had actually been one of the
best days of their lives.

Though *of course* they didn't tell each other that.

The next night, it didn't snow again – and the next day
all the children went back to school.

And, as chance would have it, just before break, Danny actually had a lesson with Mr Trapper. But halfway through the lesson something rather awful happened. Danny was just sitting in his chair, when *suddenly* Mr Trapper shouted at him.

"Higgins – are you *slouching***?"**

"Well, I suppose I might have been, though I didn't know I was, sir."

"DETENTION.
I'll see you in here at break."

Deep inside his chest, Danny felt the saddest he'd ever felt.
Everything from yesterday *melted* away, like snow in the sun.

And once again
he felt
completely
alone.

At break time, as had happened a *hundred* times before,
Danny sat at one end of the detention room and Mr Trapper sat at the other.

Then, as *always* happened, Mr Trapper wandered down after five minutes
to check that Danny was **actually** doing homework and not just doodling.

And Danny knew he was in **BIG trouble**,
because he *had* been doodling and **not** doing homework.

And Mr Trapper reached into his pocket to take out the **DETENTION** book.

But when he took his hand out – it *wasn't* the **DETENTION** book at all.

It was a piece of paper that Mr Trapper **unfolded** – and *unfolded* and *unfolded* again – to show Danny what he had been working on.

It was the most *wonderful* thing that Danny had ever seen.

And Mr Trapper wanted a lot of advice about it.
Because they were

The
Snow Day
Boys . . .

and, when the time came,
they had an important job to do . . .

So, exactly a year and a day after this story began,
on December the 5th, it snowed *again*.

All night.

Really hard.

And it was definitely

Snow Day 2.

And *absolutely* **nobody** went into school. Well . . .

. . . *almost* **nobody.**

ULTIMATE IGLOO DESIGN

© Trapper/Higgins 'The Snow Day Boys'

The End